D0132416

This Book donated by
Pacific
Northwest
Booksellers
Association
PNBA
Rural Library Project

THE MIAMI GIANT

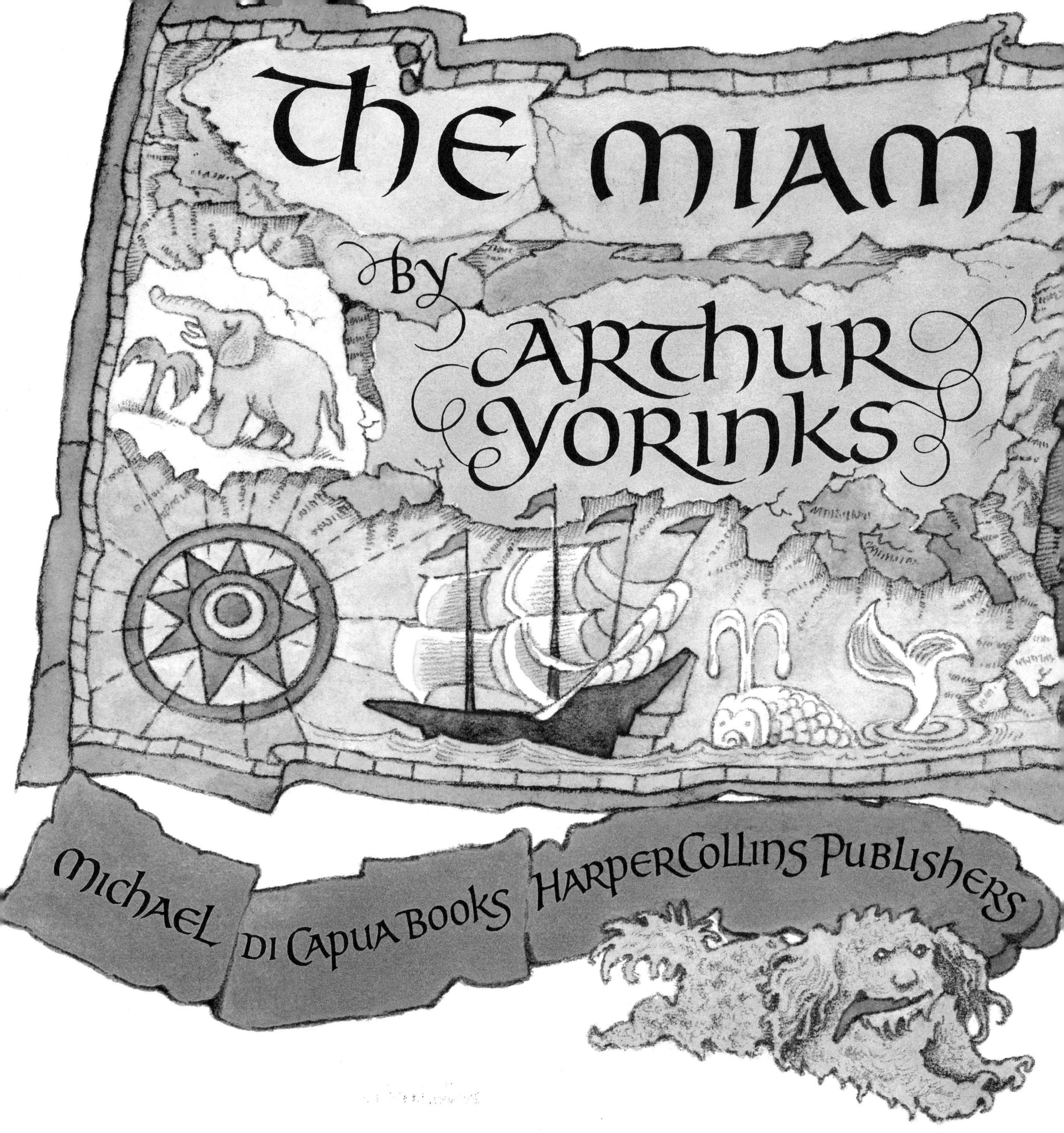

THE MIAMI
BY
ARTHUR
YORINKS
MICHAEL DI CAPUA BOOKS
HARPERCOLLINS PUBLISHERS

GIANT
PICTURES
BY MAURICE SENDAK
EUREKA! I FOUND IT!

Library of Congress catalog card number: 94-79526
Printed in the United States of America
Hand lettering by Jeanyee Wong
First edition, 1995

FOR BONGO AND RUNGE

BON VOYAGE!
AND DON'T BE A STRANGER
TRAVEL EXPENSES

AMID GREAT POMP, GIUSEPPE GIAWEENI

LEFT ITALY TO LOOK FOR CHINA.

IT WASN'T EASY.

THERE WAS FOG.

THERE WAS RAIN.

AT LAST, GIAWEENI SPOTTED LAND.

IT WAS MIAMI.

MAY-HEM-MEE?
SO I
SWERVED
A LITTLE

STILL, GIAWEENI WAS BRILLIANT. FOR THERE, IN MIAMI, HE MADE A STUNNING DISCOVERY. A LOST TRIBE OF DANCING GIANTS!

The
mishbookers
of miami

LEFT TO THEMSELVES FOR CENTURIES, THE MISHBOOKERS LED A SIMPLE, PRIMITIVE LIFE.

THEY ATE. THEY SLEPT.
THEY WENT BOWLING. WHAT A FIND!

HEY, MISTER! ME GIUSEPPE
GOD BLESS YOU
MAMA MIA! YOU SPEAK ENGLISH
GRR!

WHAT ELSE? THE NAME'S JOE, JOE MISHBOOKER
WE COME FROM FAR ACROSS THE SEA
SNIFF
SO HOW ABOUT A BITE?
THIS GUY IS STUPENDO!

AFTER A NICE BUFFET, GIAWEENI SHOWED THE MISHBOOKERS THE WONDERS OF THE MODERN AGE.

THE GIANTS, IN TURN, SHOWED OFF THEIR OWN ACHIEVEMENTS.

BEADS
COCONUT HEADS
COMFORTABLE BEACH CHAIRS
MOLTO STUPENDO! I MUST BRING ONE BACK ALIVE!

SO GIAWEENI APPLIED SOME FRIENDLY PERSUASION.

ARE YOU KIDDING? I'LL MAKE YOU A STAR!
JOE STARTED PACKING.

THAT VERY NIGHT

THEY HOISTED ANCHOR AND SET SAIL.

BACK IN ITALY, GIAWEENI RENTED A PALAZZO.

THEN HE HAD A TAILOR MAKE JOE A NEW SUIT.

HE EVEN HIRED A PROFESSIONAL TRAINER

TO GET HIM IN SHAPE FOR HIS DEBUT.

In April, in Paris, Giaweeni proudly

UNVEILED THE MIAMI GIANT.

JOE DANCED THE MISHBOOKER GAVOTTE

AND THE AUDIENCE JUST WENT WILD.

IN FACT, THEY FLED!

BUT JOE KEPT RIGHT ON DANCING.

PANDEMONIUM ENSUED. GIAWEENI TRIED

DESPERATELY TO CALM THE CROWD.

BUT IT WAS TOO LATE.
THE POLICE
DROPPED A BRICK ON JOE'S HEAD.

JOE, SPEAK TO ME!
SPEAK TO ME!
MAYBE NEXT TIME
I'LL JUST TELL JOKES

SO GIAWEENI BROUGHT JOE HOME. AND WITH A LITTLE MELON, HE RECOVERED NICELY.

Then the great explorer bid his friend farewell and went on to discover Boca.

And the mishbookers?
Some say they moved to Long Island,
but this is not a proven fact.